THE PADAWAN MENACE

ADAPTED BY ACE LANDERS
BASED ON THE SCREENPLAY BY MICHAEL PRICE

SCHOLASTIC INC.
NEW YORK TORONTO LONDON AUCKLAND
SYDNEY MEXICO CITY NEW DELHI HONG KONG

ISBN 978-0-545-40450-1

12 11 10 9 8 7 6 5 4 3 2 11 12 13 14 15/0

PRINTED IN THE U.S.A. 40
FIRST PRINTING, SEPTEMBER 2011

S THE CLONE WARS RAGED ACROSS THE GALAXY, A GROUP
F PADAWANS WERE ON A CLASS FIELD TRIP . . .
MARI
LIAM
lightsaber
AFICIONADO

JEDI TEMPLE
SCHOOL DISTRICT
. . . BUT THEIR REAL ADVENTURE WAS ABOUT TO BEGIN.

THE PADAWANS HAD ONE MORE PLACE TO VISIT — THE GALACTIC SENATE!

AWWW!
BUT WE WANT EXCITEMENT!
JEMPA

VO DROIDS NAMED C-3PO AND R2-D2 WERE THE GROUP'S SPECIAL TOUR GUIDES.
TOUR GUIDE

IDDENLY, YODA FELT A DISTURBANCE IN THE FORCE.
LEAVE YOU, I MUST. A GRAVE THREAT TO THE REPUBLIC, I FEAR.
DA HURRIED TO THE SENATE ID LEFT THE ROIDS TO WATCH IE PADAWANS.
WAIT! I'M A PROTOCOL DROID, NOT A SUBSTITUTE TEACHER! PUT ME DOWN!

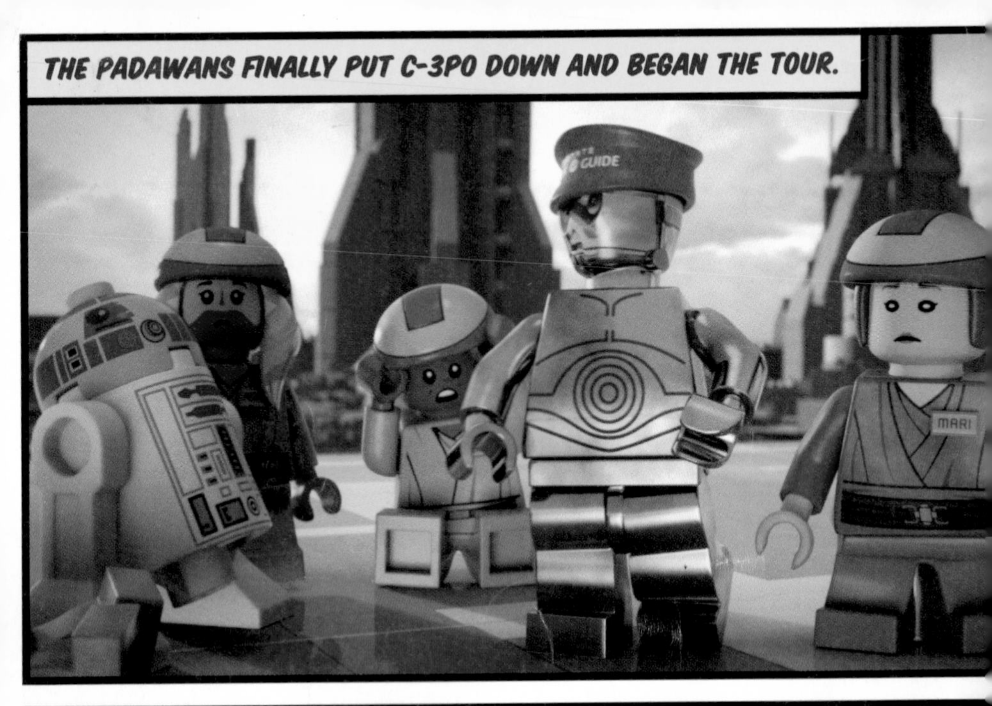
THE PADAWANS FINALLY PUT C-3PO DOWN AND BEGAN THE TOUR.
GUIDE
MARI

AS THE GROUP ENTERED THE SENATE, A MYSTERIOUS BOY SPIED ON THEM.
THIS SURE BEATS THAT ORPHANAGE!

HE BOY SNEAKED PAST THE GUARDS . . .

. BY PRETENDING TO BE A PADAWAN.
SENATE CHAMBER
HEY, WHERE DID THAT KID GO?
AWESOME!
IAN

IAN WASN'T THE ONLY ONE HIDING. ASAJJ VENTRESS, AN EVIL SEPARATIST AGENT, STOOD IN THE SHADOWS.

SAJJ CALLED DARTH SIDIOUS TO SHARE SOME NEWS.
I HAVE STOLEN THE REPUBLIC'S SECRET BATTLE PLANS.
YOU HAVE DONE WELL, VENTRESS.

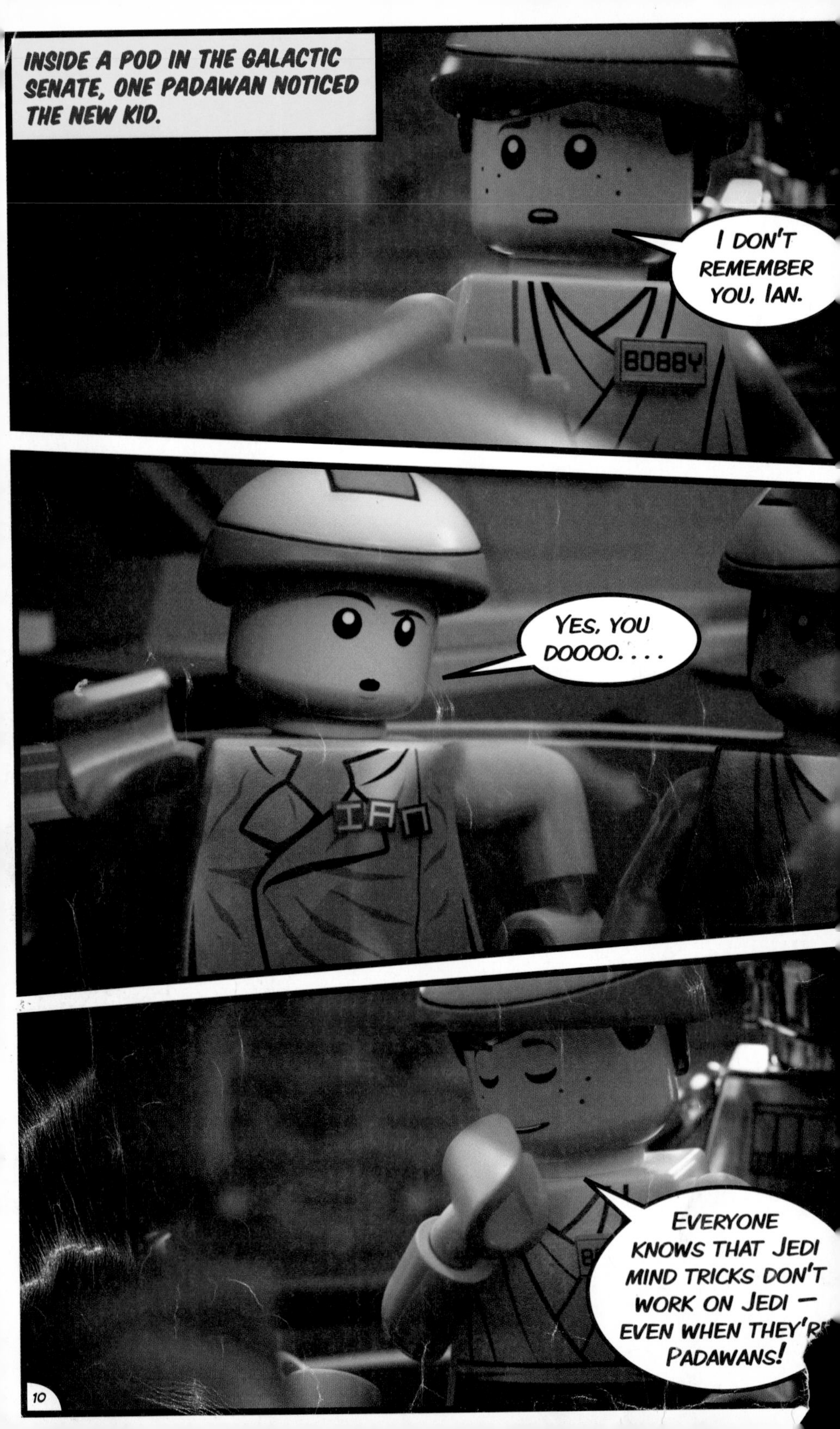
INSIDE A POD IN THE GALACTIC SENATE, ONE PADAWAN NOTICED THE NEW KID.
I DON'T REMEMBER YOU, IAN.
BOBBY
YES, YOU DOOOO. . . .
IAN
EVERYONE KNOWS THAT JEDI MIND TRICKS DON'T WORK ON JEDI — EVEN WHEN THEY'R
PADAWANS!

HE GUARDS WERE STILL LOOKING FOR IAN. HE TRIED TO
SCAPE BY REWIRING THE PADAWANS' SENATE POD.

MEANWHILE, YODA HAD FOUND THE DISTURBANCE IN THE FORCE. IT WAS ASAJJ.
TIRED OF BEING RIGHT EVERY TIME, I AM.

AS THE BATTLE RAGED, THE PADAWANS DASHED TO SAFETY.
TOTALLY AWESOME!
OH, MY STARS! TO THE BUS!

WHILE YODA AND ASAJJ DUELED, A BATTLE DROID ESCAPED WITH THE SECRET BATTLE PLANS.

SING THE FORCE, YODA TRAPPED THE EVIL ASAJJ . . .

. AND CHASED AFTER THE BATTLE DROID WITH CLONE COMMANDER CODY.
SECRET BATTLE PLANS, THAT DROID HAS!
I'M ON IT!

THE PADAWANS ESCAPED TO THE BUS — BUT THERE WAS NO DRIVER!

LUCKILY, R2 COULD FLY THE SHIP.
I CAN'T FLY THIS THING!

THE BATTLE DROID BLASTED OFF WITH THE STOLEN PLANS.

YODA AND CODY JUMPED INTO THE CLOSES SPACESHIP.
FOLLOW HIM, WE MUST!

N SPACE, THE STAR BUS RAN INTO ENEMY SHIPS.
OH, DEAR! ARTOO, GET US OUT OF HERE!
ODA AND CODY WERE ALSO IN FOR A SURPRISE.
HEY, HOW'S IT GOING?
HUH?
HEN YODA'S SPACESHIP BUMPED INTO THE STAR BUS AND
NOCKED IT THROUGH THE HYPERDRIVE BOOSTER RING. . .

CHILDREN, FASTEN YOUR LAP RESTRAINTS.
OH, NO!
. . . SENDING THE PADAWANS INTO HYPERSPACE!

THE STAR BUS CAME OUT OF HYPERSPACE AND CRASH-LANDED ON TATOOINE.
GSSSHH!

AWESOME!
YAY! LET'S DO THA AGAIN!

BUT THE SHIP WAS DAMAGED IN THE CRASH. THE PADAWANS WERE STRANDED
LOOK AT OUR SHIP! HOW COULD YOU LET THIS HAPPEN?
BLUR

MEANWHILE, YODA CHASED THE BATTLE DROID TO THE ICE PLANET HOTH.
TRACK THAT DROID THROUGH THE SNOW, WE MUST.
I'VE GOT A BAD FEELING ABOUT THIS.

CODY AND YODA SPLIT UP TO SEARCH FOR THE DROID.
HOW OLD ARE YOU, A MILLION?
TO KNOW MORE THAN YOU, OLD ENOUGH I AM, HMM!

AT LEAST KNOW HOW TO TALK NORMAL, I DO.

ACK ON TATOOINE, C-3PO, R2-D2, AND
HE PADAWANS LOOKED FOR A NEW SHIP.
YOU YOUNGLINGS STAY HERE WHILE I FIND A PILOT IN THIS CANTINA. DON'T TOUCH ANYTHING!

T THE YOUNGLINGS HAD OTHER PLANS.
LIAM

WHEN C-3PO RAN TO STOP THEM . . .
GREAT BANTHA BREATH! WHAT ARE YOU DOING!

. . . HE ACCIDENTALLY KNOCKED DOWN A WALL.
OH, MY! I'M TERRIBLY SORRY, MASTER JABBA.
JABBA THE HUTT WAS NOT HAP

N HOTH, YODA AND IAN WERE STILL SEARCHING FOR THE BATTLE DROID. THEY ERE GETTING COLD.
TO KEEP VARM, STICK OUR HEADS IN THIS ANIMAL'S GUTS WILL WE.
GROSS!
DDENLY, THE BATTLE DROID LEAPED OUT OF THE UNTAUN! YODA STRUCK IT DOWN WITH HIS LIGHTSABER.
BATTLE PLANS
WHOA! SECRET BATTLE PLANS! THAT WAS EASY!
PLANS

BUT IAN SPOKE TOO SOON. DROIDEKAS SURROUNDED THEM.
BLAST THEM!

YODA DEFLECTED THEIR BLASTS WITH HIS LIGHTSABER.

THEN IAN JUMPED ONTO A DROID AND REWIRED IT.
YEE-HAW!

N AND YODA GALLOPED BACK TO THEIR SHIP.
AW MAN, THE SHIP IS BROKEN!

DA USED THE FORCE TO CREATE A NEW ONE.

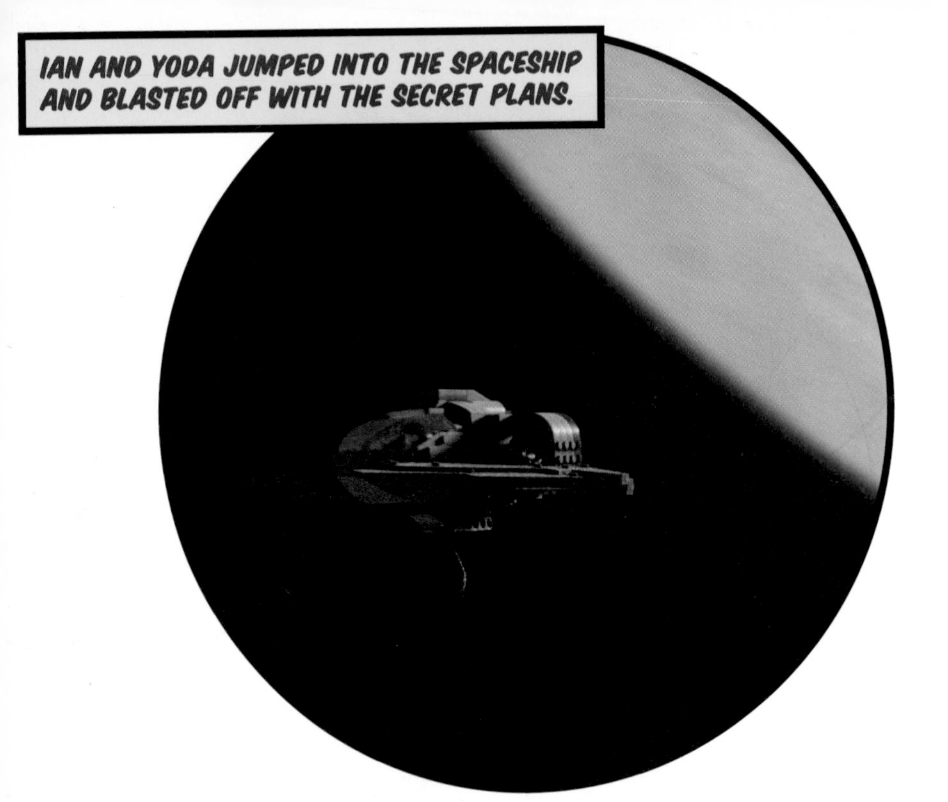
IAN AND YODA JUMPED INTO THE SPACESHIP AND BLASTED OFF WITH THE SECRET PLANS.

BUT THEIR MISSION WASN'T OVER. THEY RECEIVED A DISTRESS CALL.
MASTER YODA, THE YOUNGLINGS ARE IN DANGER!
RESCUE THEM, WE WILL.

TATOOINE, JABBA WAS SPEAKING TO A CROWD
CREATURES. C-3PO TRANSLATED HIS ORDERS.
DOPA DROI WAMMA JABBA!
THESE DROIDS WILL FOR INSULTING JABBA BY FIGHTING EACH OTHER . . . ?!
OH, MY! I DON'T WANT TO FIGHT MY BEST FRIEND!

3PO RUSHED OVER TO THE PADAWANS, WHO WERE LOCKED BEHIND BARS.
I'M SO SORRY! I'M A FAILURE!
BOBBY

BUT AGAIN, THE YOUNGLINGS HAD OTHER PLANS.
YOU'RE NOT A FAILURE. YOU'RE A HERO! BREAK THOSE PILLARS WITH YOUR WEAPON!

C-3PO BROKE THE PILLARS, AND THE ROOF CRASHED DOWN ON JABBA.

THEN R2-D2 FREED THE PADAWANS!

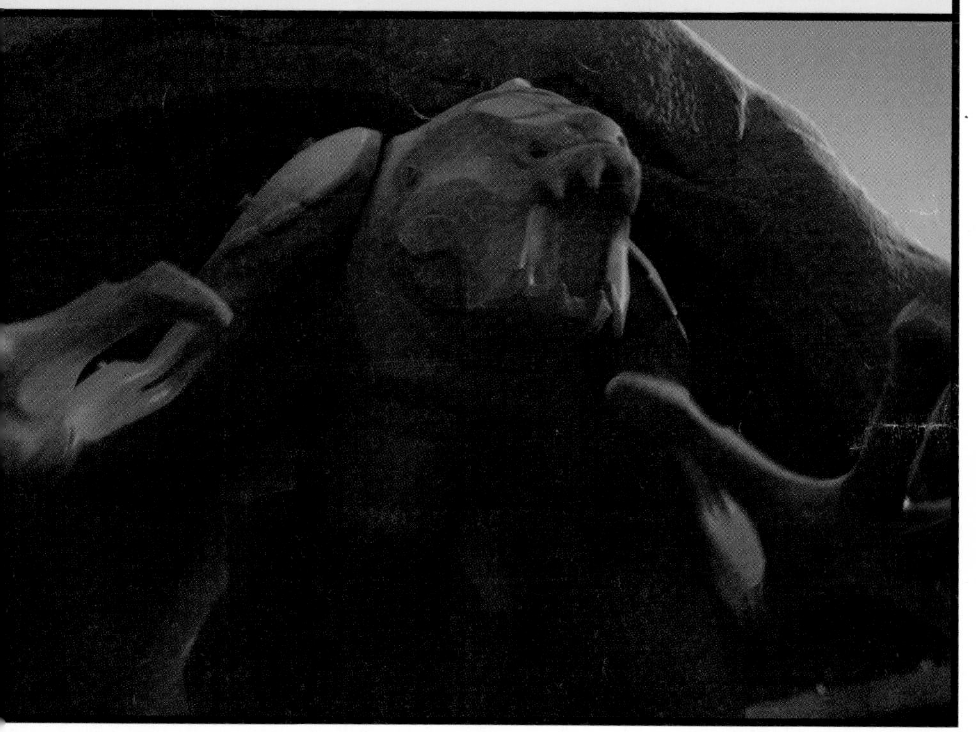
FORE THEY COULD ESCAPE, A FEROCIOUS RANCOR RUSHED OUT OF THE PALACE!

IT HEADED STRAIGHT FOR THE PADAWANS!
RUN AWAY!
PALACE

SUDDENLY, A GIANT MAGNET PICKED UP C-3PO. IT WAS YODA AND IAN, COMING TO THE RESCUE!
WHOA!

THE PADAWANS GRABBED ONTO C-3
AND THE SHIP LIFTED THEM INTO TH
SKY. THE YOUNGLINGS WERE SAVED!
WELCOME
JABBA's
PALACE

A, IAN, C-3PO, R2-D2, AND THE PADAWANS
DED BACK TO THE JEDI TEMPLE.
I AM A HERO! I ONLY WISH MASTER YODA COULD SEE ME NOW.
SEE YOU I COULD, F SITTING N ME YOU ERE NOT.
EXCUSE ME, SIR!

WHEN THEY ARRIVED, THERE WAS A BIG CELEBRATION FOR IAN AND THE BRAVE PADAWANS.

YODA GAVE IAN A MEDAL OF HONOR.
MANY ADVENTURES IN YOUR FUTURE HAVE YOU, YOUNG IAN.

THANKS,
BUT MY NAME IS NOT
IAN — IT'S HAN . . .
. . . HAN SOLO.
HAN

A PLEASURE
TO MEET YOU,
MASTER SOLO.
THANKS,
GOLDYPANTS.
HAN

ALL WAS WELL AGAIN IN THE REPUBLIC.
JEMPA
AWESOME!